katie

the Revolting holiday

Also available in the KATIE series
THE REVOLTING BRIDESMAID
THE REVOLTING WEDDING
THE REVOLTING BABY

THE REVOLTING
hOLIDAY

MARY HOOPER

ILLUSTRATIONS BY
FREDERIQUE VAYSSIERE

BLOOMSBURY

Published in Great Britain in 2008 by Bloomsbury Publishing Plc
36 Soho Square, London, W1D 3QY

First published in the UK by Blackie Children's Books, 1994

Text copyright © 1994 by Mary Hooper
Illustrations copyright © 2008 by Frederique Vayssiere

The moral rights of the author and illustrator have been asserted

A CIP catalogue record of this book is available from the
British Library

ISBN 978 0 7475 8614 2

All papers used by Bloomsbury Publishing are natural, recyclable products made
from wood grown in well-managed forests. The manufacturing processes conform to
the environmental regulations of the country of origin.

Typeset by Dorchester Typesetting Group Ltd
Printed in Great Britain by Clays Ltd, St Ives Plc

1 3 5 7 9 10 8 6 4 2

www.maryhooper.co.uk
www.bloomsbury.com/childrens

chapter one

'Well, what I think,' said Mrs Bayleaf, without waiting to be asked what she thought, 'is that we ought to take a nice little cottage somewhere quiet in the country.'

Everyone tried to look politely interested but I felt the beginnings of panic. Imagine being stuck in the middle of nowhere with *her*.

We were gathered together in our sitting room to plan a family holiday. There was Mum and Dad and me, my sister Helen and her husband Christopher, and Mr and Mrs Bailey, who were Christopher's mum and dad. There might have been more room if Mrs Bayleaf (as I always called her) hadn't been filling two seats on the settee just with herself and her shoulder pads.

'Just think,' Mrs Bayleaf went on, 'the sound of birdsong in the morning and the smell of new mown hay! Cows trotting down the lane and –'

'I don't think cows trot, dear,' Mr Bayleaf interrupted.

She glanced at him – that's all she had to do. He shrank into our fireside chair.

'Cows trotting towards the farm . . .' she resumed expansively, 'going home for milking with their big placid faces almost smiling . . .'

She turned her big, placid, almost-smiling face to us. It was unfortunate that she was wearing black and white, really, because I think the same thought occurred to everyone at the same time. Anyhow, Dad got a fit of coughing and had to go out of the room.

'Well, then,' Mum said swiftly. 'And what other ideas have we got for the holiday?'

'Disneyland,' I said.

No one took any notice. Mr Bayleaf said something about a golfing holiday and Helen said she fancied a week on a small island in Greece.

'Disneyland,' I said again, and I added pointedly, 'It was me who got you the money for the holiday, after all . . .'

When I'd been looking after Helen and Christopher's baby, Emily, I'd taken her to be

photographed in a studio and she'd ended up being featured in a Sunday magazine whose editor had paid Helen and Christopher a lot of money. That's why we were having the holiday – because Christopher thought everyone should benefit from the windfall – not because anyone liked Mrs Bayleaf or wanted to go anywhere with her. Far from it.

'We've told you before, Katie,' Mum said to me, 'there just isn't enough money for us all to go to Disneyland.'

'I could go on my own,' I offered.

'Personally, I'd like a restful week at a hotel with a swimming pool,' Mum said.

'Rather fancy sailing, myself,' Dad said, coming back with a tray of coffee cups.

'That's an idea,' Christopher said. 'And I wouldn't mind learning to play squash properly, either.'

Mum counted off on her fingers. 'So we've got a country cottage, a hotel, a Greek island, golf, sailing, and a learning-to-play-squash holiday.'

'And Disneyland.'

'Six very different ideas,' Christopher said.

'Seven,' I put in, but of course they ignored me.

'So, to be completely fair and impartial,' Christopher said – he's a teacher, he always speaks like that – 'we ought not to choose any of them. We ought to go for something entirely different.'

'Well, what do we all actually want from a holiday?' Mum said, and everyone started telling her.

'It's no good,' she said after a few moments. 'Everyone wants different things. We're never going to be able to please everyone.'

'So how about just pleasing the person who got you the money to go,' I muttered.

'I've just had a thought,' Helen said slowly.

'What about a holiday camp? At one of those we'd all be able to do different things.'

'Count me out!' Dad and Christopher said together, and I think Mr Bayleaf might have said it too but Mrs Bayleaf suddenly crooned, 'What a good idea!' and he didn't dare.

'It's not normally the sort of holiday I'd choose, but I do believe they can be quite fun,' Mrs Bayleaf informed us. 'They have ballroom dancing classes and popular entertainers in the evening and all sorts of jolly competitions. Glamorous Granny is a favourite, I believe.' She winked at Mum. 'You and I will be deadly rivals for that one, eh!'

Mum looked horrified — she won't even go in for the mums' egg-and-spoon race on school sports days. 'I think I'll leave that one to you, Beattie,' she said, 'but I do think a holiday camp is quite a good idea. There'll be lots going on to keep Katie amused, too.' She looked at me severely. 'It might keep her out of trouble.'

'Oh, indeed,' Mrs Bayleaf said, and she sort of jigged from side to side on the settee and made a ludicrous face at me. 'Teenage disco dancing, eh, Katie!'

I pretended not to see her.

'And there'll be things to amuse Emily, too,' Helen said. 'Yes, I think that'll be best all round. We can cook for ourselves if we want to . . .'

'Cedric does a marvellous barbecue!' Mrs Bayleaf said. 'Don't you, Cedric?'

But before Cedric could speak up, Christopher interrupted. 'Before we all commit ourselves completely, may I venture to suggest a new angle: a men's break-away holiday.'

Mr Bayleaf brightened up considerably. 'You certainly may!' he said.

'Cedric!' Mrs Bayleaf said. 'Don't be beastly to Beattie!'

'Sounds good to me,' Dad said very quickly. 'You women can do your womanly things . . .'

'And we men can do our manly things,' Christopher finished. 'We can have a sporting activities week somewhere.'

I saw Mr Bayleaf's eyes gleam at the thought of offloading Mrs Bayleaf for a week.

'If we're all separate it'll hardly be a family week away,' Helen objected.

'But on the other hand,' Mum said, 'it could be

11

a lot more restful. Yes, I think it's a good idea. You men go away together.'

Mrs Bayleaf rallied. She liked everyone to think she was chilled and free-thinking. 'Well, yes, I suppose an all-girls-together holiday might be quite nice . . .'

I felt my heart sink dreadfully at the thought of a whole week of Mrs Bayleaf: Mrs Bayleaf from when I cleaned my teeth in the morning to when I cleaned them at night. Continual Bayleaf . . . torrents, floods, *oceans* of Bayleaf.

'Can Flicka come with us?' I asked.

'Sorry!' Mum and Helen said together.

'There won't be enough money,' said Helen.

'You get into enough trouble on your own without having Flicka around,' put in Mum.

'Anyway, you'll make friends there,' Helen said. 'They have clubs, don't they?'

'Lots of super teenage goings-on!' Mrs Bayleaf trilled. 'Dancing round your handbags to music from the hit parade!'

I smiled grimly, wondering if we'd both make it to the end of a week.

Mrs Bayleaf clapped her hands. 'We must all

have new outfits! I simply insist that everyone comes to see me in Cocktail and Continental Cruise Wear and chooses a special glittery dress!'

'Mmm . . .' Helen and Mum said together, looking uneasy.

'Do they do tracksuits?' I asked.

Mrs Bayleaf ignored me and smiled fatly at Mum. 'I'm really beginning to feel very enthusiastic about this holiday!' she gushed. 'You, me, Katie, Helen and Emily! What a lovely, gossipy girlie time we're all going to have!'

'Er . . . yes . . . we certainly are,' said Mum in a faint voice.

chapter two

'Oh, look, Katie!' Mum said, pointing towards a square, flat-roofed building. 'There's the Kids' Klub.'

We'd just arrived and were standing at the window of our chalet, looking out on the wonders of the holiday camp.

'Kids' Klub,' I said in disgust. 'You needn't think I'm joining that.'

'It might be fun . . .'

'So might tying two balloons to your ears and pretending you're a rabbit.'

'Oh dear,' Helen said, looking. 'They've spelt it with two Ks. Good job Christopher can't see it.'

Christopher, Dad and Mr Bayleaf had gone off on their men's holiday the night before, Mr Bayleaf seeming rather hysterical. 'Light-headed with relief,' I'd overheard Mum describe him to Helen.

As we stood in the chalet looking around us, Mrs Bayleaf puffed through the door, struggling with a cabin trunk balanced on a set of wheels. 'Most inadequate, these luggage trolleys,' she said. 'Simply useless for anyone with more than the absolute minimum of clothing.'

Helen, Mum and I stared at the buckled wheels of the trolley, then we stared at the size of the trunk. Mum rolled her eyes at Helen.

We were in what they called the reception room of our chalet – really the hall. There were also three bedrooms, quite a big bathroom and separate loo, and a kitchen big enough to eat in.

Emily, who'd been fast asleep in her buggy with her log tucked beside her, woke up. Emily never went anywhere without her log. She'd even had it in the magazine photograph. Mrs Bayleaf flew to her side, leaving the trunk wedged across the doorway.

'Did the Boofums wake up den?' she cooed.

Helen rolled her eyes at Mum.

'Granny thinks that baby Emily is too hot in all those clotheses,' Mrs Bayleaf said, struggling to take off Emily's jumper.

This time Mum and Helen rolled their eyes at each other.

'About the bedrooms,' I said. 'Can I have the one nearest the door?' All the better to get in and out without being detected . . .

'There are only three bedrooms. Two of us will have to share,' Mrs Bayleaf said, cooing at Emily and squishing up her lips so they looked like a monkey's bottom.

'I can't share. I have to have Emily in with me!' said Helen quickly.

'I can't, either. I . . . I think I'm getting a cold

16

and I'm going to snore very loudly all night,' I put in.

'I . . .' began Mum, just as Mrs Bayleaf interrupted to say to her, 'Looks like you and me together! Don't suppose we'll get a wink of sleep with all the gossiping we're going to do!'

Heaving a sigh of relief, I escaped into my room and began to unpack. This didn't take long; I just chucked big things on the bed or backs of chairs and small things along the windowsill and on the table. Once this was done, I peered out of the window towards where it was all happening. This holiday was the only one I was getting so I had to make the most of it.

Apart from the Kids' Klub, I could see the swimming pool (with chutes), a small fairground and various signs saying things like *To the Ballroom, Starlite Nite Club* and *Shopperama*. Zooming around everywhere were the staff, all looking like children's TV presenters in their bright yellow dungarees.

Mrs Bayleaf put her head round my bedroom door, looked round and emitted a high-pitched scream. 'Burglars!' she said.

'What?'

'You must have had burglars in here!' she said. 'Look at the state of the place!'

'Oh no,' I explained, 'my bedrooms always look like this.'

She shook her head sadly. 'Dear, oh dear. My Christopher was always such a tidy child.' She waved a metal object at me. 'I came to say that I have a small travelling iron with me, should any of your little dresses need pressing after the journey.'

I looked at her steadily. 'What is a *dress*?' I

18

asked, and she shook her head sadly again and disappeared.

A little bit later Mum came in to say that they'd all unpacked and were now going to look round the camp; would I like to come with them?

'No, thanks,' I said, thinking that I'd rather die than be seen to be going round with my sister, my mum and someone who looked like an Auntie from Hell.

As soon as they'd all disappeared I decided to go and have a look at the Kids' Klub. I didn't for one minute intend to actually *join*, I just thought it would be something to do. When I got home I could tell my friends how twee and awful it had been and how everyone had begged me to join but I'd absolutely refused.

When I got inside there, though, it actually didn't look too bad. It was just one big room with a tuck shop and a stage and a list of activities on the wall, with interesting things like *Midnight Trek* and *Scuba Diving* written up. Before I knew what was happening a bouncy sort of woman wearing a badge saying *I'm Hannah* had taken down my name and stuck a badge on me saying

I'm a Kids' Klubber.

'I'm not sure that I . . .' I began.

'Oh, don't be shy!' she said. She beamed at me toothily. She was wearing yellow dungarees and a baseball cap back to front in a failed attempt to look cool. 'You'll enjoy yourself with us. We have a *wonderful* time!'

Well, I thought, quickly weighing things up, no one at home need ever know; it would be something to do – and best of all, Mrs Bayleaf couldn't join.

I mooched around a bit and went to put my name down for some of the activities listed. There were a couple of boys and a few other girls mooching about too — all of them younger than me. I thought this was a bit off at first, but then I realised that this meant I could be in charge; help organise them . . .

On the stage were twin CD decks, and Hannah asked me to be DJ. 'Saturdays are changeover day and kids come in and out all afternoon,' she told me.

By four o'clock there were twenty or so there. I'd just put on another selection of tunes and was telling an interested crowd how excellent I was on the trampoline, when a girl about my age marched in, said to Hannah, 'I'll do the DJing again this week, shall I?' and went and changed my CD.

The small crowd of little girls I'd been impressing immediately left me and went over to her. Hannah said, 'Ah, Antonia. I didn't realise you were staying another week!'

'Oh, we're having such a marvellous time everyone voted to stay on!' said the Antonia person. She sat down on the edge of the stage swinging her legs, surrounded by an admiring crowd. She was very brown and had blonde hair which could have been highlighted. She also had a silly gaspy voice and little twinkly stars in pierced ears.

'I had such an exciting day today!' she said in the gaspy voice. 'I had a windsurfing lesson and I stayed up straightaway and went absolutely miles. The instructor said I was a natural.' She went on and on about this for a bit and then she suddenly noticed me. 'Oh, we've got someone my own age this week,' she said. Her voice fell. 'How nice.'

'This is Katie,' said Hannah. She turned to me. 'This will be Antonia's second week. She's been a wonderful help to me.'

'I love being with the younger ones,' Antonia said with a nauseating smile. 'People say I've got a special bond with them. And I like being DJ here, too.' A frown crossed her delicate features. 'Talking of being DJ – whoever put on the awful music that was playing when I came in?'

'She did!' one of the small boys said accusingly, pointing at me.

'Really?' Antonia said.

'You actually like the stuff that's on now, do you?' I asked incredulously. 'Where I live, it went out years ago.'

'Where *I* live it's back in,' said Antonia. She jumped off the stage and went over to Hannah. 'Has my diary got its gold cover yet?'

'It certainly has,' said Hannah. From out of her desk drawer she brought a gold-covered book, which she held up. 'Most of you are new this week, so I'll explain what the Kids' Klub diary is all about. We've got lots of activities for you to try, and we also give you a notebook and ask you to fill it in every day.'

'What for?' a small girl interrupted, and Antonia hushed her. 'Quiet while Auntie Hannah's talking, sweetheart,' she said, patting the child's head.

I was nearly sick on the spot.

'We ask you to write down not only everything that happens while you're here, the good deeds, the competitions you've won, the sporting prizes you've achieved, but also everything your family party has done, too. At the end of the week you'll have a complete record of your holiday — and the best diary each week wins a super prize!

'I'll just pass the diary around so you can see Antonia's work,' Hannah went on. 'Take care with it, won't you? It's one of the nicest we've ever had and it'll go into our big competition at the end of the year.'

When the diary came round to me I passed it straight on, pretending to yawn slightly, but looked over the other kids' shoulders and swiftly read bits of it:

Dad won the tug-of-war.

Mummy made a gorgeous hat for the Make a Hat competition. She won, of course, and everyone thought I looked beautiful in it!

This afternoon I won the Little Miss Lovely competition and posed by the pool for photographs for our local paper.

Later, Mummy said I must remember those who are not as fortunate as me, so went to help out at the Red Cross station. Gave an exhausted old man a glass of water.

It went on like this for pages. And there were little sketches and coloured illustrations and photographs of her wearing sashes saying *Little Miss Lovely* and *Miss Fancy Dress*. There were also pictures of all her family winning prizes; from what I could see they'd won practically everything in the whole camp.

'I want *wonderful* diaries from everyone!' Hannah said, handing out identical blue notebooks.

'But don't put yourselves out too much,' Antonia laughed merrily, ruffling a little boy's hair. 'Because I intend to win *this* week's prize, too!'

I laughed merrily back. *Over my dead body*, I thought, and went back to the chalet to start my diary.

Saturday's Diary

Arrived this afternoon with my family and straightaway rushed to join the Kids' Klub — after all, that was one of the main reasons we came to the camp! It looks such fun and I can't wait to join in all the competitions and activities that Hannah is arranging for us. She's so nice.

I helped her with the younger children until a girl called Antonia came in and took everything over, including the music. Some of the others thought Antonia was too bossy and pushy by far but I said to give her a chance; she might be the sort who is just covering up shyness. (And pigs might fly.)

It's Antonia's second week here — you can see that because the sun has bleached her hair

(I think it's the sun!). She proceeded to tell us what she'd been doing all day in great detail — a couple of the younger ones fell asleep but I managed not to. After that we all had to look at her last week's diary, and I could tell straightaway that Antonia doesn't go in for false modesty — she believes that if you're good at something, you should say so!

I expect it will be difficult competing against someone who has been everywhere and won everything, but I might have a bit of a try at winning the Diary prize myself this week . . .

chapter three

Just before lunch I wandered back to our chalet, kicking the gravel and feeling bitter and twisted.

Mum, who was sitting on the little porch in the sun, put down the magazine she'd been reading and looked at me sternly. 'Where have you been?' she asked. 'Mrs Bailey wanted us all to go to the swimming pool together.'

'That's why I disappeared,' I said. 'I couldn't face the thought . . . I just know she's got a great big swimming costume with a huge bow on the front and a pleated skirt in shiny red satin.'

'Shiny green satin, actually,' Mum said. 'But where did you go?'

I knew she'd have to know. 'The Kids' Klub,' I muttered.

Mum smirked. 'Oh, you *did*, did you? In spite of saying that you wouldn't go within ten miles of it? In spite of saying you wouldn't go if we paid you because it would be all Blue Peterish and . . .'

'They forced me to join,' I interrupted. 'They heard I was here and wanted someone like me to get things moving.'

'Oh yes?' Mum said. 'Well, next time tell me before you disappear. Why are you looking so fed up, anyway?'

'Because *she* won the It's a Knockout competition,' I said dourly.

'It's not whether you win or lose, but how you run the race,' Mum said automatically. 'Anyway, who did?'

'Antonia,' I said heavily.

'What a pretty name,' Mum said, picking up her magazine again. 'I'm pleased you've made a friend so quickly.'

'I haven't made a friend. She's awful. I hate her.'

But Mum had suddenly found an article entitled: *Looking Good Over 40!* 'That's nice . . .' she murmured.

'She put prickly things in my sack so I couldn't jump in it, and let the air out of my ball so it wouldn't bounce properly and moved the ladder so I couldn't find it to climb.'

'She does sound fun,' Mum said, reading on. 'You'll have to bring her over for lunch.'

'I told you, I hate her,' I said irritably. Mum didn't reply and I peered through the window of the chalet. 'Where's Helen?'

'Gone to take Emily for a walk and to book us in for the Starlite Club tonight – there's a cabaret and the first of the big competitions on.'

'What sort of competitions?'

She looked up from the magazine. 'Oh, everything you can think of – Knobbly Knees, Large and Lovely, Limbo, Sumo Wrestling and there's a Dads and Lads contest – whatever that is. Everything!'

'And which ones are you going in for?' I asked with interest. I had to get our family winning things somehow. I'd discovered that there were five people in Antonia's family: her, her mum and dad, sister and brother – and there were five of us, too, if you counted Emily. OK, we obviously couldn't go in for the men's Knobbly Knees or the Dads and Lads, but Mrs Bayleaf should be a cert for the Large and Lovely. Or at least the Large bit of it.

'Me?!' Mum said. '*Me?!* I'm not going in for any competitions. I just want to sit and watch everyone else make fools of themselves.'

'You told me I ought to join in everything!' I said. 'You told me the more you put in, the more you get out.'

'That's different,' Mum blustered.

'Coo-ee!' came a call, and Mrs Bayleaf appeared round the corner. 'I *have* had a lovely walk!' She flopped into a chair next to Mum. 'I've made all sorts of discoveries and had a lovely nose around.' She looked at me archly. 'And I even spied a certain little girl in the It's a Knockout competition!'

I looked at her coldly.

'You didn't do very well, did you, dear?'

'Nor would you!' I began heatedly. 'Nor would you if someone was –'

'Such a nice girl seemed to be winning everything. A very pretty girl with long blonde hair.'

'Oh, that must be Katie's new friend,' Mum said. 'Antonia, her name is.'

'She's not my friend!'

'A pretty name for a pretty girl!' Mrs Bayleaf said. 'And I'm pleased that you've found such a

nice girlie friend.' She looked me up and down. 'Just what you need, if you don't mind me saying.'

'She may look nice,' I said darkly, 'but she's actually a very dangerous escaped criminal.'

Mrs Bayleaf gave a shriek of alarm.

'Take no notice, Beattie,' Mum said calmly. 'That's Katie's idea of a joke.'

After a sandwich lunch, during which Mrs Bayleaf told everyone how many It's a Knockout games I'd lost and how talented/pretty/popular Antonia looked, I started to work on Mum. I was desperate for her to go in for the Fancy Hat competition that afternoon.

'It's only for adults,' I said wheedlingly. 'You won't have to perform or anything. All you've got to do is make a hat. You did tell me that the more you put in, the more you get out . . .'

After ten minutes or so of this sort of thing she caved in, saying something about doing anything for a quiet life.

The posters said that the competition started at two o'clock, but when we got to the small hall dead on that time, Antonia's mum (same streaked hair) was already there, seated at a table with the

most enormous pile of flowers in front of her. Ant, as I'd decided she'd just hate to be called, sat demurely by her mum's side, wearing her It's a Knockout winner's rosette. There were other small tables placed around the hall, and at the front was a long trestle table holding a handful of dead-looking grasses.

'That blonde woman got here early and pinched all the best flowers,' a woman whispered to Mum. 'That's how she won it last week.' She indicated the trestle table. 'The rest of us have got to make do with what's left.'

Everyone turned to stare at the grasses and a rebellious muttering started.

'Lovely afternoon, ladies!' Ant's mum smiled at us sweetly. We could only just see the top of her smile – the rest was lost beneath what looked like half the Chelsea Flower Show.

'I don't think I'll bother with the competition,' Mum said to me. 'I'll just pop off and have a swim.' She lowered her voice. 'I must say, I don't think it's very nice of your friend's mum to –'

'I keep telling you, she's not . . .' I began, but Mum was going out of the door. I hauled her back. 'Just hang on,' I said. 'Give me two minutes!'

Mum joined the other entrants in a rebellious mutter and I went over to Ant's table.

'What lovely flowers! I love roses, don't you, Ant? And you get a particularly interesting kind of spider on these . . .' I made a pouncing movement into the pile. 'Missed him! Really good specimen – big and hairy with little red eyes. Ooh, there's another!'

There was a startled shriek from Ant and a matching one from her mum. They jumped up from the table and started brushing down their clothes furiously.

'Just a sec!' I cupped my hands as if to pick a huge spider off Ant's neck and they both moved back from the table at the speed of light.

I turned towards Mum and the other entrants. 'Lots of flowers here for whoever wants them!'

Everyone swarmed in on Ant's table and within a minute the pile of flowers had been distributed around to the other ladies. Ant and her mum came back to four dead daisies and a couple of dandelions.

'Now, ladies!' A yellow-dungareed man with a badge saying *Hi, I'm Kevin!* came in carrying a pile of straw hat shapes. 'I see you've got your flowers already!' he said heartily. (They were always hearty.) 'Well, I want you each to take one of these straw hats, go to your tables and come out fighting!'

I wasn't allowed to help, but I did give Mum one strong hint. 'You want a hat that's seriously over the top,' I whispered. 'Think Mrs Bayleaf.'

Mum won.

Sunday's Diary

I didn't do quite so well as I'd hoped in the It's a Knockout this morning but that didn't bother me a bit. That's not what competitions are all about, is it? I think the important thing is just to take part. What I always say is:

It is better to have run and lost,
Than never to have run at all.

Some of the others thought that someone had been trying to ruin my chances deliberately, but I thought that was ridiculous. As if anyone would do that even if they did win everything themselves last week and didn't want to be beaten this week!

In the afternoon my mum won the Fancy Hat competition. Below is a sketch of the winning hat, which the judge said was the best he had ever seen. Ever. And much better than last week's one.

Not being funny or anything but I don't think it's fair that people are allowed to get to the hall early and pinch all the flowers. Not mentioning any names, of course, and not meaning anyone in particular, but <u>is it fair?</u>

chapter four

'It was nice that your mum won the Fancy Hat competition,' Ant said the next day. 'The judges thought my mum's was lovely, actually – they really liked the uncluttered, simple look – but Mum turned down the prize. She didn't think she should win it two weeks running.'

'That was nice of her, Ant,' I said. 'That was nearly as nice as me letting you win the It's a Knockout contest.'

'Did you?' she said. 'I didn't realise.'

'I could have wiped the floor with you!' I said. 'When you're an international athelete like me, though, you don't think it's right to win against ordinary people.'

'Funny,' she said, looking me up and down. 'You don't look like an international athlete. They're usually strong and muscular, but you're quite scrawny.'

'I'm honed for total fitness,' I said.

We were lounging about outside the Kids' Klub, waiting for Hannah to come along and busy us into our next activity. As we waited, Ant dug into her pocket and distributed boiled sweets to all her hangers-on. 'My brother and dad are going in for the Dads and Lads competition this morning,' she said to me. 'I know they'll win.'

'Why's that?' I asked. 'Have they bribed the judges?'

She crunched loudly. 'No, it's all on personality,' she said. 'We're the life and soul of the party types,

40

you see. All my family have great personalities.'

'*Have* they?' I asked disbelievingly.

Hannah arrived to tell us about that morning's *wonderful* Kids' Klub competition.

It was for girls only, and you had to swim three lengths of the pool using different strokes, show you knew how to lifesave and put someone in the recovery position, do a couple of dives and then parade round the pool a bit. Apart from the parading bit it sounded all right and we'd gone over to the small pool and I was just changing into my swimsuit, when Hannah announced that the actual name of it was the Little Miss Holiday Princess competition.

I stopped dead with one leg in my swimsuit. What if anyone at home found out I'd been in for a Little Miss Holiday Princess competition? My street cred would be ruined; people would point fingers at me; dogs would bark at me in the street.

'It's not a beauty competition,' Hannah said. 'It's just to show you're a good all-rounder.'

While I hesitated, Ant, in a padded-with-bosoms, shiny pink swimsuit, pushed past me and dived straight into the pool, amid applause.

I pulled myself together and put in my other leg. No one knew me down here – and if anyone found out I'd say I'd been tricked into going in for it; I'd just been walking through the camp and someone had kidnapped me and forced me to enter . . .

I did all right on the swimming and diving bits, but went seriously downhill when it came to the parading bit because I felt so soppy and also because I was only wearing my stretchy, navy-blue chain store number. Ant, naturally, was wearing pink sparkly flip flops and not only the padded-

with-bosoms swimsuit, but a matching swimming hat covered all over in pink nylon flowers. Tasteless or what?

We'd hauled ourselves out of the pool and were parading around and it was only when I saw all the judges nodding and smiling towards her that I realised that they went in for tasteless. *Tasteless* was exactly what they liked.

I thought quickly.

'Lovely new swimsuit, Ant,' I said.

'Mmm,' she said smugly. 'It's a designer one.'

'Pity it's transparent.'

'What!?'

'You can see right through it. Specially when you're standing full in the sun.'

'Aagghhh!!' She doubled up, clutching bits of herself, grabbed a towel and ran straight into the changing rooms.

I went up to Hannah. 'Isn't it a shame — Antonia's decided to withdraw,' I told her, and as all the other girls entered for it were younger than me and none of them knew how to lifesave properly, I won. I took my Little Miss Holiday Princess sash home and put it at the bottom of my suitcase.

That same morning, unfortunately, Ant's dad won the Archery competition and then he and her brother won the Dads and Lads. Slightly despondent, I went back to the chalet to look at my lot and see what I could persuade them to go in for.

'I think you'd be great at the Limbo competition,' I said to Helen.

'What – bending down under a stick, showing my knickers?' Helen said. 'Certainly not. Anyway, I don't really agree with all this competitiveness. You wouldn't get me putting Emily in for a Bonny Baby competition, for instance.'

'No, of course not,' I said. I braced myself to look at Mrs Bayleaf. She was wearing a dress as bright and as big as a patchwork quilt and had sunglasses with pointy twirly sparkly bits at each side.

'Wouldn't you like to go in for something, Mrs Bailey?' I asked politely. Perhaps a stained-glass window look-alike competition, I thought. I looked down at the list I'd made. 'There's Clay Pigeon Shooting, Snooker – or what about the Archery?'

'None of those are quite me, dear, are they? I'm more the power woman type than the sporting type. Isn't there anything for a glamorous older woman to enter?'

'There might be — if we knew any glamorous older women!' I said, and then I laughed loudly to pretend it was a joke.

I looked at my watch. 'Can I take Emily for a walk?' I asked Helen.

She looked at me suspiciously. 'What for?'

'Just to give us some fresh air. A quiet walk around the camp grounds,' I said. 'You're always telling me I don't see enough of her.'

'Do let her, Helen,' Mum said. 'She's trying to be helpful.'

'Exactly,' I said, putting on my saintly face.

Emily was sitting in her buggy on the porch with us and Mrs Bayleaf swooped upon her. 'Is sweetest babykins going outsies with her auntie Katie, then? Or shall *Granny* take her walkies?'

Helen got up immediately. Emily was picked up, changed, her face was wiped. The instructions came thick and fast. 'Keep the sunshade up . . . Don't go too far . . . Don't give her any sweets . . . Don't stop to talk to anyone.'

Still wearing the saintly face, I set off — and

headed straight through the fresh air towards the dining hall, where the Bonny Baby competition was being held. This was one thing that Ant's family couldn't enter . . .

But Ant was already there, holding a big bald baby.

I looked at her crossly. 'Where did you get *that*?'

She smirked. 'He's a sort of cousin.'

'How d'you mean — *sort of*?'

'He's in the chalet next door. But he's family for the purposes of the competition.'

'That's not fair,' I said. 'Anyone could go round

adopting people for competitions. I could have adopted a dad and a lad.'

'Why didn't you, then?'

I scowled at the baby. 'Where's its hair?' I asked, and she ignored me and put a white bonnet over the baby's bald head, tying it under its fat chin.

I got Emily out of her buggy and took her over to sit on a long table with the rest of the babies, next to Ant and her baldy, who was playing with a bright blue ball. All the other babies had something in front of them to keep them amused, too, so I got Emily's log out of the buggy. After a few

moments the judges appeared and started walking down the table and everyone started clucking at their babies to make them laugh.

The judges slowly made their way along, asking daft questions. I suppose they had to ask things, because all the babies looked more or less the same – some were just fatter or balder than the others. I was hoping they'd make Ant take off her one's hat, but they didn't.

When they got to us, I told them Emily was my niece, my *real* niece and not a *sort of* niece, then a blue-rinsed lady judge asked why Emily was playing with a log. I was just about to explain that she preferred logs to teddies, when I had a better idea.

'We can't really afford teddies,' I said wistfully. 'You see, Emily's father is . . . gone . . .' I looked down at the ground and gulped noisily, hoping that she wouldn't realise that I just meant he'd gone on a men's break-away sports week. I lowered my voice. 'It's very sad. We . . . we don't like to talk about it.'

'No. No, of course not, dear,' Blue Rinse said hastily, patting my arm. 'How tragic. So poor baby here has only a piece of wood to play with . . .'

'That's right,' I said with a sigh. 'There's not much money for toys . . . We just have to get along the best we can.' I looked longingly at the large stuffed orange tiger on the top table that was the prize. 'It would be lovely to win today . . .'

Blue Rinse sniffed into a hanky. 'We'll see, dear. We'll see . . .'

Fifteen minutes later I arrived back at the chalet with a sash saying *This Week's Bonny Baby* up my sweatshirt and a large orange tiger under my arm.

'Wherever did you get that?' Helen said as I dropped it on the table.

'It's just a little something I got for Emily,' I said lightly.

'But you know she won't play with anything except a log!'

'Well, it'll be a souvenir of the holiday,' I said.

Mum picked it up. 'Look at the size of it!' she said. 'This must have cost quite a bit. Fancy you spending all that money!'

'It's just a little something . . . You always say I don't take enough notice of her,' I murmured.

As I went off into my bedroom to do my diary, I

saw Mum and Helen exchange incredulous glances. As I closed the door I heard Mum say in a stunned voice, 'You know, sometimes I think we misjudge Katie . . .'

Monday's Diary

Had a wonderful morning winning the Kids' Klub Holiday Princess competition. I really didn't expect to win because the other girls were so good, but funnily enough the judges thought I was even better. My mum always says that talent will out and I suppose she's right.

After preparing a light lunch for my family I took my little niece Emily to the Bonny Baby contest. She is my actual niece actually, not like Some People who borrow babies from chalets next door and not mentioning any names but Some People actually do this.

Much to my surprise we won the competition. One of the judges — a lovely woman with blue hair — was so taken with Emily that she had tears in her eyes as she handed over the prize, which was a big stuffed orange tiger.

chapter five

'Turrah!' trumpeted Mrs Bayleaf from behind the chalet door. 'Are you ready for me?'

I groaned. No one could ever be *really* ready for Mrs Bayleaf.

'Yes! Come and give us a whirl!' Mum called, trying to enter into the spirit of the occasion.

Mrs Bayleaf moved majestically through the chalet door and out on to the porch, resplendent in flame-coloured chiffon. Downwards from massive padded shoulders hung trails of red, yellow and orange scarves, which swirled and floated out as she moved; swished all round her head was a big matching turban. The general effect was of a well-stoked bonfire suddenly come to life.

Mum and Helen started clapping. Emily burst into tears and had to be picked up.

'Well!' Mum breathed.

'Stunning . . .' said Helen.

'What a sight!'

They all looked at me. 'A magnificent sight,' I amended quickly, for Mrs Bayleaf, who'd refused to enter the Large and Lovely, was preparing for the Glamorous Granny contest that evening and had to be encouraged at all costs.

'This is my "Light My Fire" number,' Mrs Bayleaf said, parading up and down the porch in front of us. 'It's been a great hit this season in After Six Cocktail and Continental Cruise Wear.'

We all made appropriate murmurs. Mum's murmur drowned out mine of, 'Well, there's no accounting for taste.'

'Or there's my pink candyfloss outfit – the one I had for the wedding,' said Mrs Bayleaf. 'Or, just wait and see this . . .' and she disappeared inside the chalet again.

While we waited for the next Bayleaf experience I made a mental list of the competitions we'd won and those that Ant's family had won. The trouble was, they were winning lots of sporting things and we didn't have anyone sporty with us. Her dad had even won the Sumo Wrestling contest and though I'd put Mrs Bayleaf's name forward, she wouldn't go. If she could win the Glamorous Granny, though, that would really be something.

Five minutes later there was another trumpeting from within and Mrs Bayleaf put a leg round the door and made kicking movements in the air.

'Oooh!' Emily went as the rest of Mrs Bayleaf emerged, and I would have ooohed too except the sight of her had quite taken my breath away. From head to toe she was encased tightly in a slinky chainmail tube of silver sequins which glittered and shone in the sunlight. She looked like a giant haddock on legs.

'This,' Mrs Bayleaf announced grandly, 'is from our showbiz range. We call it the "Royal Variety Performance" number.'

She started twirling round extravagantly and making the porch shudder, crying 'I'm a chorus girl!'

We sat in stunned silence.

'Well, what do you think?' she asked. 'Which outfit shall it be?'

'I think,' Mum said, rallying slightly, 'that you'll knock 'em dead in that one.'

'That's just what I thought,' said Mrs Bayleaf, and she turned to go in, giving us a back view like two Christmas turkeys fighting to get out of their cooking foil.

After tea, Mrs Bayleaf went off for a last-minute appointment in the Health and Beauty Club, so we said we'd see her later at the judging.

Later, once Emily was settled with her baby-sitter, we made our way to the ballroom. The place was packed. All the judges were on a raised platform at the back of the stage and, in honour of the occasion, they wore not only their yellow dungarees, but also yellow blazers.

Before the Granny bit, though, we had to sit through the Knobbly Knees contest. This was won by Ant's brother, who'd drawn little faces on his knees with a felt-tip pen which he wriggled up and down to make the judges laugh. An example of the whole family being *personalities*, I suppose. Ant was sitting near us with her dad and sister, and they all hooted and screeched every time her brother wriggled his knees. I told Mum and Helen not to dare to smile.

'Have you fallen out with your new friend, then?' Mum asked.

I ignored her.

'You'll make it up tomorrow, I expect,' Helen said. 'You often get these little hiccups at the beginning of a friendship.'

'She's not my . . .' I began, but stopped as the orchestra struck up *'You must have been a beautiful baby . . .'* and the Glamorous Granny contestants were announced. The third one out was Ant's mum.

'How can she be a granny?' Mum wanted to know. 'She's got her children with her and none of them look old enough.'

'She isn't a granny,' I said. 'The whole family

just come here to go in for the competitions. If there was a dog show they'd all dress up as Jack Russells and enter that.'

'Hmm. Bit much,' Mum said.

'Go and complain!' I urged.

'Don't be silly,' Helen said. 'And anyway, it wouldn't be very nice to tell on your new friend, would it?'

I ground my teeth but didn't say anything because I didn't want to miss Mrs Bayleaf's entrance.

As if anyone could. The other Glamorous

Grannies minced on and offstage in their ordinary long dresses: pinks and blues and blacks and whites – but when Mrs Bayleaf sashayed on in silver, the whole place went mad. Well, there was so *much* of her and she was all shimmering. With Mrs Bayleaf you really got value for money.

'She's got a wig on!' screeched Helen to Mum.

'She's wearing at least three pairs of false eyelashes!' Mum croaked back.

'Bayleaf, Bayleaf, ra, ra, ra! Bayleaf, Bayleaf, she's a star!' I shouted.

There were fourteen contestants and the judges

narrowed the field down to five, then three, but really it was over before it had begun. Mrs Bayleaf won by popular demand – and Ant's mum didn't even come in the first three.

Afterwards, wearing a sash saying *I'm a Glamorous Granny* and a silver tiara, Mrs Bayleaf came to sit among us.

While we offered congratulations, she smiled regally about her. 'Thank you . . . thank you so much for your support . . .' she said, giving a royal family wave towards people on nearby tables.

'Well done, Beattie,' Mum said.

'I've ordered four framed copies of me being presented with my sash,' said Mrs Bayleaf. 'There will be one for everyone.'

'How lovely!' said Mum.

'I knew I'd win, of course,' she confided. She lowered her voice. 'The secret is to bring a little glamour into people's lives . . . touch their drab existence with sunshine.'

Basking in the Bayleaf sunshine, I smiled smugly towards Ant. Why, Mrs B really wasn't too bad. Given time, I might even get to like her.

'Of course,' she went on archly, 'we mustn't forget the other star in the family, must we?'

'What — me winning the Fancy Hat competition?' Mum laughed. 'Oh, that was nothing.'

'No, I mean our Little Miss Holiday Princess!' said Mrs Bayleaf, nodding towards me so that her tiara shook, and I knew that I could never like her, not ever in a hundred years.

'What's that?' Mum asked.

'What do you mean?' said Helen.

'Well, I was talking backstage to the girl who runs the Kids' Klub, and when she found out who I was, she told all,' Mrs Bayleaf said with a leer. 'There's a little girl we know who's won the Little Miss Holiday Princess competition but is keeping very quiet about it! A little girl not very far from where I'm sitting whose name begins with a K!'

Mum and Helen stared at me. 'You surely don't mean Katie . . .' Mum said in disbelief.

'Katie a Little Miss . . .' began Helen incredulously.

'. . . Holiday Princess?' gasped Mum.

I began to think that an early night might be in order.

'It wasn't actually a Holiday Princess as such,' I

blustered. 'It was more a sporting thing . . .'

'Little Miss . . .' Helen bleated.

'Holiday Princess!' Mum finished in a shriek of laughter.

'That's right,' said Mrs Bayleaf.

I got up. 'I think I'll go back and check how Emily is.'

'Dear little Emily,' said someone behind me, and I turned to see the blue-rinse person who'd judged the Bonny Baby. 'How is the lamb?'

My eyes glazed over. 'Ah . . . oh . . . fine.'

'Such a tragedy about her father,' the woman said in a low and sympathetic voice.

Mrs Bayleaf, Mum and Helen all stared at me, then turned to stare at the woman.

'But . . . Emily's father is with my husband . . .' Mum began.

Blue Rinse clapped her hand to her mouth. 'No! Don't tell me – a double tragedy in the family. How dreadful! And you've all come on holiday to get over it.'

'What?' said Mum, Helen and Mrs Bayleaf together.

I didn't stay to listen to any more. I did hear,

'Katie! Come back here immediately!' but I just carried on running.

Tuesday's Diary

This morning we all helped Mrs Bayleaf decide which of her stunning outfits she should wear for the Glamorous Granny contest. After much laughter and jollity (we are such a fun family) we chose a dress which made her look like a large and beautiful mermaid. We must have excellent taste, because Mrs Bayleaf won!

The result was only fair, really, because another woman, who shall be nameless (but the one who pinched all the flowers) isn't a grandmother! Cheats never prosper, is what I say.

After the judging, my family found out that I'd won the Little Miss Holiday Princess competition. I hate boastful people so I'd been keeping it a secret! There was more laughter and jollity as I confessed all!

There was almost too much excitement for one evening, so soon after that I decided to go back early and look after Emily.

chapter six

'Look, don't keep going on,' I said to Mum and
Helen at breakfast the next morning. I dipped a
bread-and-butter soldier into my boiled egg. 'I
don't know how that judge woman got the idea
that Emily didn't have a dad. It was nothing to do
with me.'

'It must have been!' Helen snapped, putting Emily and her log in a high-chair together. 'I don't know what you told her but it led to one of those ghastly embarrassing situations that you're always getting us into.'

'I simply told her that Emily's father had gone on holiday . . . it wasn't my fault that she got the wrong end of the stick.'

'She thought we were too poor to afford a toy for Emily – and that's why she won the prize!' Helen sniffed so hard her nose went white. 'I've a jolly good mind to give it back – Emily hates the ghastly tiger anyway!'

'You mustn't do that,' Mum interrupted. 'It would just create more fuss. No, the less said the better.'

Helen glared at me. 'Well, Katie, this is the last holiday of mine you ever come on,' she said. 'Everywhere you go there's trouble.'

'It's not my . . .' I began, but we all stopped as Mrs Bayleaf edged into the room wearing a pair of jeans, a plunge-neck black T-shirt and the sash announcing she was a Glamorous Grandmother.

We said good morning and then just sat there

kicking each other under the table as she poured herself a cup of tea.

'Will you . . . er . . . be wearing your sash all day today?' Mum asked delicately.

'Oh, I think so,' Mrs Bayleaf said. 'Until the end of the week, probably. I think the rest of the camp expect it, don't you?' She sipped her tea, little finger crooked out. 'And I really think Katie ought to wear her Holiday Princess sash, too.'

'I lost it,' I said immediately.

'Tut-tut, Katie,' said Mrs Bayleaf. 'Our nose will grow long if we tell lies, won't it?' She adjusted the sash and patted it. 'Besides, you should be proud of winning. Proud to be a Holiday Princess.'

'*Little Miss* Holiday Princess,' Helen put in spitefully.

'Why, I remember years ago I won a Fairy Princess competition!' Mrs Bayleaf beamed at us. 'I had a pair of wings made of net and a wand with a star on it and . . .'

I beat a hasty retreat, grabbing a few bread-and-butter soldiers on the way out, and arrived at the Kids' Klub at the same time as Ant. She had her diary in a plastic folder under her arm and looked smug.

'I've almost run out of pages – my family are doing so much!' she boasted.

I riffled through my own diary's pages and pretended to look overwhelmed by what was recorded. 'Me too!' I said. 'Although, of course, where competitions are concerned we prefer to go for quality rather than quantity.'

'Yes, people who haven't won much always say that,' Ant said. 'Done your community service yet?'

'I've done some . . .' I said cagily, not quite sure what counted and what didn't.

'This week . . . well, I think I've done something pretty special.'

I pretended not to hear the last bit, pretended to be engrossed in drawing something in my diary, but actually desperate to know what she meant. Not quite desperate enough to ask, though.

I soon found out what it was. A few of the younger kids came in and then Hannah appeared and started pinning up lists and times for the Table Tennis and Volleyball knockout competitions. Ant and I, as oldest there, started picking our teams. Suddenly, a small boy wearing purple trainers rushed in.

'Has she told you!?' he puffed. 'Has she told you about the runaway horse she stopped?'

Everyone looked at everyone else, wondering what he was going on about.

Ant got to her feet, lifting her hands as if to stop waves of imaginary applause. 'No, no – it was nothing,' she said, smiling modestly. 'I really don't want any fuss.'

Hannah came over. 'What happened?' she asked.

'Oh, I just stopped a dangerous runaway horse on the beach yesterday,' Ant said. 'Merely grabbed the reins, flung myself over its back and pulled it up.'

'How wonderful of you!' Hannah said. 'What a thing to put in your diary!'

'No . . . no, I shall hardly mention it,' Ant said. 'And please, *please* don't start referring to me as a heroine.'

'I didn't know anyone was,' I muttered.

'I know I could have ended up with two broken legs, but really . . .' she shook her head dismissively '. . . it was nothing.'

A small girl called Laura was standing next to me. She screwed up her nose. 'Well, it wasn't *much*,' she whispered to me. 'Because I was there. It wasn't exactly a *horse*, either.'

'What was it, then?'

'A donkey,' she said. 'A donkey with a straw hat on. It was doing rides on the beach and then someone with an ice cream walked past and it trotted after them. She . . .' she nodded towards Ant, 'she ran up and pulled it back. No one even knew it had gone!'

'So how come it got turned into a runaway
horse?'

'That boy with the purple trainers was there,'
Laura said. 'And he's in the next chalet to her.'

'Ah-ha,' I said. 'I see.' I looked at Laura
thoughtfully. 'Would you like a lovely orange
tiger of your very own?' I asked.

'Yes, please!' she said.

'Come and see me before we go over to the volleyball court, then.'

'No, no . . . it was nothing,' I said modestly later

that afternoon. 'Please don't make me out to be a heroine or anything.'

'But you were *wonderfully* brave,' Hannah said. 'It was real community service! I saw Laura fall in the boating pool and before I could even move you'd jumped in after her.'

'Oh, well . . .' I shrugged. 'One has to do something.'

'The water only comes up to your knees in that boating pool,' Ant pointed out. 'Laura couldn't have drowned.'

'But Katie didn't know that, did she?' Hannah put in. 'That's true bravery for you — jumping in, regardless of consequences. Wonderful!'

'Like me and the runaway horse?' Ant said eagerly, but no one answered. Her moment of glory was over; this was mine.

Keeping a heroic yet modest smile on my lips, I put a towel around Laura's shoulders. 'I'll walk Laura back to her chalet to get some dry clothes, shall I?' I asked Hannah.

'That would be wonderful.' Hannah beamed at me. 'And then hurry back to captain your volleyball team.'

I propelled Laura through the camp and towards the chalets.

'Did I do OK?' she asked. 'I had to kneel down before the water even came up to my waist.'

'You did great,' I said. 'I'll drop the tiger off later.'

'I can't bear it . . . I can't bear it . . .' I muttered under my breath, as up onstage in the Central Ballroom, Ant and her mother, father, brother and sister took yet another bow.

Beside me Mum, Helen, Mrs Bayleaf and the rest of the audience clapped and cheered. 'Whoa!' Mrs Bayleaf whooped, and I wanted to crawl under my seat.

'Very talented, your friend's family,' Mum said.

'Oh, *very*,' I said. It was talent night and we'd just sat through Ant's family yodelling, juggling, singing 'How Much is That Doggy in the Window?' complete with dog imitations, and generally making complete nerds of themselves. About the only thing they hadn't done was put on spangled suits and swing through the air on flying trapezes.

'I don't think they're finished yet,' Mum whispered to me. 'They're down for a novelty number.'

'Oh no,' I groaned. While the audience rustled their programmes and sipped their drinks I looked at Mum crossly. 'Are you sure you can't do anything?'

'Quite sure,' she said.

'Call yourself a mother? You must have some sort of talent.'

'Just a talent for putting up with you,' she said.

Mrs Bayleaf leant across Mum, squashing half the air out of her. 'Have you made up with your little friend Antonia yet?' she asked me.

I gave her a withering look.

'Well, I should do it quickly. The way her family's going they'll soon be getting their own television series.'

The band played a few notes to get everyone to stop talking and the place hushed. From the side of the stage Ant appeared with her sister. She was dressed entirely in pink and had a big brush thing wrapped around her head, and her sister was wearing exactly the same but in blue.

I made a strangled noise.

'*I'm a pink toothbrush . . .*' Ant began singing, making cutesy curtsying movements towards her sister. '*You're a blue toothbrush . . . Have we met somewhere before?*'

I got up, holding my hands over my ears.

'Where are you going?' Mum demanded. 'There's lots more to come.'

'That,' I said, making for the exit, 'is exactly what I'm afraid of.'

Wednesday's Diary

I hardly like to write this but Hannah is insisting on it, so I'd better! Today I rescued a small helpless child from drowning.

Luckily I'm proficient in life-saving so I jumped in the boating pool, hauled out poor little Laura and dragged her to the side, then proceeded to put her in the recovery position where she soon revived completely. I laughed it off when everyone wanted to sing 'For she's a jolly good fellow!' After all, I was only doing my community service — what any brave person would have done.

It was quite a day for community service because someone else stopped a trotting donkey.

In the evening we went to the talent contest. Antonia's family are so talented they could have entertained us all evening, but occasionally another competitor managed to get onstage.

chapter seven

'There's no doubt about it – they stole the show,'
Helen said the next morning.

'Mmm,' I said.

'I mean, I can't say I like all that showbiz stuff
– more like showing-off biz if you ask me – but
they've certainly got talent.'

I *mmmmed* again and passed a piece of crispy bacon to Emily, who in turn passed it to Loggy.

'So what's next, then?' Mum asked. 'What's on this afternoon?'

'The Grand Fancy Dress,' I said with a sigh.

Mum nodded towards the bathroom, where noises like an elephant at the waterhole meant that Mrs Bayleaf was cleaning her teeth. '*Someone* we know must have something to wear to that,' she said.

I shook my head. 'It wouldn't be good enough. Not *fancy* enough.'

'You need to think of something really unusual to wear for fancy dress these days,' Helen said.

'I thought of wearing a sheet and going as Cleopatra,' I said, 'but I'm not going to stand a chance. Ant's sister is going out with the theatre manager here, and he's letting their family have pick of all the proper costumes.'

'Well, that hardly seems fair,' Mum said. 'I mean, I know Antonia is your best friend and everything but it puts the rest of the camp at a distinct disadvantage.'

I noted briefly that Ant had now been promoted

to be my best friend but couldn't be bothered to protest. 'She's going as Elizabeth the First with jewels and crown and a ginger wig and everything,' I said bitterly. 'Me in a sheet with a black dustbin liner for a cloak can hardly compete with that, can it?'

'Well, hardly,' Mum said. 'Still, you're not doing it for the prizes, are you? All these competitions have just been a bit of fun for you this week . . . something to occupy you.'

'That's right,' I lied.

As far as the competitions went, I reckoned Ant and I were more or less equal. Our diaries were being judged the next day, though, and unless something drastic happened, it looked as if her family were going to win the last major competition. Mrs Bayleaf was my only hope . . .

She finished gurgling and spluttering and came into the kitchen. She was wearing a tight white sundress, which showed rather more of her bosoms than you would ever want to see.

'As it's our last day I thought I'd show off my tan!' she said.

Oh pur-lease, I thought. 'Oh lovely,' I said. I gave

a delicate cough. 'It's the Grand Fancy Dress contest this afternoon, Mrs Bailey,' I said politely. 'Are you going to go in for it?'

She shook her head, fighting to get her Glamorous Grandmother sash over her head. 'I don't think so, dear. I'll just rest on my laurels.'

I bit back saying I hoped they were jolly big laurels if they were going to take her weight.

'One major competition is quite enough,' she went on. She reached for a pile of toast and started buttering it thickly. 'Besides, I'll be fully occupied in the Health and Beauty Club all this afternoon.'

'Going for a 50,000 mile service?' I asked.

'Katie!' Mum said warningly.

'Just a joke, Mum!'

'I was thinking of going there for a manicure,' Mum said, 'but I couldn't get booked in. What are you having done, Beattie?'

'The works!' said Mrs Bayleaf.

'What's the works?' I asked.

'Face pack, reflexology, underwater massage and seaweed wrap!' said Mrs Bayleaf. 'Treat yourself, Beattie, I said. You deserve it.'

'Oh,' I said. *Seaweed wrap*, I thought. *Interesting* . . .

I spent the morning beating Ant in the Diving competition. Afterwards I was about to challenge her to a staying-under-the-water-longest competition but she went off, saying she had to decide what wig, jewels and accessories to wear with her fancy dress.

'It's different for you,' she said with a sneer. 'It doesn't take very long to wrap a sheet round you.'

'What makes you think I'm wearing a sheet?' I said.

'Oh – everyone wears them,' she said. 'That's all they do – drape a sheet round them and come as a Roman centurion, a ghost or Cleopatra.' She flicked her hair out of her eyes. 'While I'm getting ready I'm going to work out what to spend my diary winner's book tokens on.'

'Dream on!' I called after her.

I already had the beginnings of an idea, and after lunch I scouted around the camp buildings for a while, finding out where everything was. As luck would have it, the Health and Beauty Club was situated right next door to the Central Ballroom, where the Grand Fancy Dress was going to be.

By then I'd decided I wouldn't bother to go in for it myself. With Ant's family in all their borrowed gear, normal people weren't going to stand a chance. Luckily I had someone who wasn't normal to enter on our behalf . . .

At three o'clock I peered into the ballroom where the contestants were lining up ready, then went next door to the Health and Beauty Club.

There was a force field of perfume and hair lacquer around the reception desk, but I forced my way through it and addressed a woman wearing a yellow overall with yellow plastic flowers in her hair.

'Excuse me, but I've got an urgent message for Mrs Bailey,' I said. 'Where can I find her?'

The woman smiled at me; her front teeth all had lipstick on. 'What's the message, dear?' she said. 'I'll pass it on.'

'It's a personal message,' I said firmly.

She looked down at the big book on her desk. 'Mrs Bailey is actually in the middle of her sea-weed wrap at the moment.'

That'll do nicely, I thought. 'It's highly confidential.' I lowered my voice. 'You see, she's an important foreign diplomat.' I didn't even cross my fingers – well, she worked in *Continental* Cruise Wear, I reckoned that was almost the same as being a foreign diplomat.

'Really?' The woman pointed down a corridor. 'She's down there in the third cubicle on the right.'

On the way down the corridor I worked out what I was going to do, then I tapped on the door. Once in, I stood still for a moment, just goggling.

Mrs Bayleaf was sitting in a plastic moulded chair, wearing what looked like a very big baby's green stretch suit with bits of sea-weedy stuff slapped all over it. Her hair was slicked down with what looked like thick green conditioner and on her face was a pale green face pack. There was an eye mask across her eyes.

I stopped, mesmerised by the sight before me. It was as if I'd suddenly found myself in a film about aliens landing; it was all I could do not to give a horrified shriek and run out.

I cleared my throat. 'Mrs Bailey?' I said.

'Who's that?'

'It's me – Katie,' I said. 'I've come to lead you to safety.'

'*What?*'

This time I did cross my fingers. 'A . . . er . . . small fire has broken out in reception,' I said. 'They've asked everyone to wait in the annexe while they deal with it.'

'I can't go like this!'

'You'll have to,' I said firmly. 'It's safety precautions. The whole place has got to be evacuated.'

'But I –'

'I'll help you,' I said. 'Just leave everything in place – eye mask and everything, and I'll walk you out of the fire exit and into the annexe.'

'Well, really!' she said. 'I hope I get a good reduction for all this inconvenience.'

It was but a short walk out of the fire exit, down a corridor and backstage in the ballroom.

'Just wait here a sec,' I said. 'I'll see where we've got to go next.'

'What a fiasco,' she snorted.

I rushed into the wings, past dozens of Cleopatras, ghosts and Roman centurions, and

beckoned to the yellow-suited compère. 'There's an important last-minute entry!' I said breathlessly.

'Everyone's been on, love,' he said. 'We're about to choose the winners now.'

'Please!' I said. 'We're late because it's such a fantastic and really unusual costume – it took a lot of putting on.'

'Well . . .' He waggled his finger at me. 'Just this once, then!' He flourished his clipboard. 'Who have you got and what are they dressed as?'

I took a deep breath. 'I've got Mrs Bailey,' I said, 'and she's entering as a cartload of spinach.'

Thursday's Diary

This morning my family all discussed the Grand Fancy Dress, but in the end decided not to go in for it as Some People would be wearing, not jolly home-made outfits, but proper ones from the theatre, which doesn't seem very fair to me. But still, I suppose that's up to them if they want to cheat (again).

Later in the morning I spent some time beating Antonia in a diving competition. She was very good — but I was better, if I may say so.

In spite of Some People cheating, fun-person Mrs Bayleaf decided to make a last-minute entry to the Grand Fancy Dress and stole the show with her interpretation of a cartload of spinach. It just goes to show that people can win things even if they aren't going out with the theatre manager!

chapter eight

The next morning we all overslept and, as no one could be bothered to cook breakfast, we went to the Top of the Morning coffee bar to have hot chocolate and Danish pastries.

'I really am most confused,' said Mrs Bayleaf, in a bayleaf-green velour tracksuit.

'I'm not surprised,' Mum said, and she looked at me searchingly. She'd cross-examined me the night before but I hadn't given anything away.

'Lovely morning!' I said sunnily. I picked a glacé cherry from my Danish and passed it to Emily, who began to roll it up and down her tray.

Helen removed it. 'We've got to be out by ten tomorrow morning,' she said, 'so we really ought to pack tonight.'

'There's the prize-giving to go to at eight o'clock,' I reminded her, 'when I get to receive first prize for my diary.'

'As if you'd let us forget.'

'*Most* confused,' Mrs Bayleaf repeated. 'I just can't understand it. I mean, there I was having my seaweed wrap when Katie came along and wanted to evacuate me — something about a fire.'

'Which luckily just turned out to be fire *practice*,' I put in.

'And then when we eventually got back to the beauty salon Katie told me that I'd won the Grand Fancy Dress contest!'

Mum looked at me very searchingly indeed, but I didn't even flinch.

'I mean – I didn't even know I'd gone in for it!' Mrs Bayleaf cried.

'I don't think,' I said carefully, 'that it was actually fancy dress they meant. Not the *fancy* sort of fancy dress.'

'What do you mean, dear?' Mrs Bayleaf asked, looking even more confused, and Mum sucked in her cheeks and narrowed her eyes at me, ready to pounce if I faltered or hesitated.

'I think they meant it as a sort of general, over-all prize,' I explained. 'For dressing the fanciest – you know, the *smartest*, they mean – all week.'

'Oh, well . . .' Mrs Bayleaf said, preening slightly.

'That's what I understood.'

'I see.' Mrs Bayleaf looked down at herself. 'Well, that's all very nice,' she went on, 'but I think I'll stick to wearing my Glamorous Grandmother sash. The colour's more me.'

Back in the chalet, later, I put the last-minute touches to my diary, which had to be handed in to Hannah at midday. I stuck in all my photographs, did some extra illustrations, then added a couple of letters – one from Laura, thanking me profusely for saving her from certain death by

drowning, and one which was supposed to be
from Emily, saying she was pleased that I let her
go in for the Bonny Baby contest. I did think of
adding one from Mum saying what a wonderful
daughter I was, but decided that it might be taking things too far.

I added some flourishy bits around the pages
and finished it, positive that it was going to be
better than Ant's. I'd already decided what to buy
with my book tokens, and was now getting
excited about the 'surprise' prize, which Hannah

had proudly announced someone had just donated. Just suppose it was a week's free holiday for me and a friend – I could come back with Flicka and we could have a really great time, completely Bayleaf-free.

I arrived with my diary at the Kids' Klub at twelve.

'I'm only waiting for your friend Antonia's one now,' Hannah said, patting the pile of books on the desk in front of her. She lowered her voice. 'Actually, the contest is only between you two older girls. The younger ones haven't done half the *wonderful* things that you two have done.'

'Oh, I've been having such a good time that I haven't really bothered to think about the diary,' I said, carelessly flinging it on top of the pile. 'What's important is to join in and play fair, isn't it?'

'That's right,' Hannah said, 'but I'm sure you've done a wonderful diary.'

'Oh, I've just scribbled in a few odd bits and pieces,' I said lightly.

Hannah consulted her watch. 'I wonder where Antonia's got to? It would be dreadful if she didn't get her diary here on time, wouldn't it?'

'Shall I go and see?' I asked. 'Perhaps she's forgotten the time and I could collect the diary and drop it off for her . . .' Into my mind came a vision of me collecting it and dropping it off into the boating pool.

Just then, though, Ant ran in and laid her diary reverently on Hannah's desk. It was tied round with a blue satin bow, and into the bow was tucked a small posy of flowers.

'Special delivery!' Ant said, all sweet and gaspy. 'And the flowers are for you for looking after us so

well all week!'

Hannah was quite overcome. 'How truly wonderful!' she said. 'No one's ever given me flowers before.'

Grr . . . I thought. 'Oh, haven't mine arrived yet?' I said. 'I hope they haven't got lost.'

'Well, it's all been very nice here,' Mum said that evening as we waited for Mrs Bayleaf, 'but all the relentless jollity does get me down a bit. I'm looking forward to a nice quiet night in with a book.'

'All the activity has been wasted on Emily,' Helen said. 'She probably hardly noticed we were away.'

'She's been really good with her babysitters, though,' Mum said. 'I expect she . . .'

Mum stopped dead, everything stopped dead, as Mrs Bayleaf made one of her entrances, looking like sunset over the prairie.

'I thought I'd wear my "Light My Fire" number tonight,' she said. 'It seemed a shame to bring it all this way and not use it.'

'Oh, quite,' Mum said. She shot me a look and I shut my mouth. I'd got away with quite a lot this holiday; I knew better than to push my luck.

We set off for the Central Ballroom, Mrs Bayleaf's flames fluttering and flying around her and making her look like a large, walking firework display. A group of interested children followed at a distance.

I walked as far away from her as possible so that people wouldn't think she was anything to do with me. Only one more day of her! All I hoped was that we could off-load her as quickly as possible in the morning and she wouldn't have to come all the way home with us.

As she fluttered, she waffled on about Bliss's department store and how simply invaluable she was as a manageress.

I switched off, and started wondering when I would have to put up with her again. Maybe not until Christmas. At any rate, whenever she came I was going to be out.

We went in the ballroom and sat down right at the front – all the better to go up and get my prize. The younger children's prizes were being given out first, then the Kids' Klub Diary prize, and then the finalists for all the sporting events had to go up for their miniature silver cups.

While we waited, Mrs Bayleaf, who was sitting in between Mum and me, started warbling on about the qualities you needed in After Six Cocktail and Continental Cruise Wear. I sat, hardly listening, wondering how I could persuade Mum to let me and Flicka come back for a week on our own. I knew she'd say I was too young and make me wait until I was thirty-five — either that or insist on coming along too . . .

'Of course, I get lots of young girls writing in from their schools asking about a career in fashion. They want to work in designer clothes — and they all want to be as successful as me!' Mrs Bayleaf warbled.

'And now we come to this week's Kids' Klub Diary prize!' the man in the yellow top hat announced, and I sat up straight and tried to ignore the continuous drone from beside me.

'What I tell them is that to get where I am you've got to be dynamic!' she hissed.

'Hannah told me,' Yellow Hat said, 'that there were two outstanding entries; two wonderful entries from Miss Katie Wilkins and Miss

Antonia Smythe-Brown — and when I saw them for myself I had to agree with her.'

Out of the corner of my eye, I saw Ant flick back her streaked hair and prepare to collect her prize. The cheek of it! I didn't dare move. Mrs Bayleaf nudged me and went on in a hoarse whisper, 'So because all you young girls are interested in clothes, I decided that it would be nice to donate a little extra prize this week . . .'

Suddenly I heard her — and suddenly was struck with horror. Frozen, dumbstruck, *transfixed* with horror. What did the woman mean? But before I could ask her . . .

'And although it was very, very close, we've decided to award the diary prize to Miss Katie Wilkins!'

Mum nudged me. 'That's you! Well done!'

'I . . .'

Mrs Bayleaf prodded me — it was like having a garden fork stuck in my ribs. 'Aren't you the lucky girl!'

In a daze, I walked up the steps on to the stage.

Yellow Hat smiled smarmily. 'Katie wins lots of book tokens — and this week, a super extra prize!

95

We've got a special lady with a very important job here this week, and she's offered a week's work experience at her lovely store, learning all the tricks of the fashion trade in . . .' he consulted a piece of paper, '. . . After Six Cocktail and Continental Cruise Wear!'

Polite clapping swept across the ballroom and Yellow Hat slapped me on the back. 'Katie, what a lucky girl you are!'

Mrs Bayleaf, the Revenge. A whole week, with her, in After Six Cocktail and Continental Cruise Wear . . .

'Oh, yes,' I said in a strangled voice, 'I'm dead lucky.'

'You can take your week any time you like in your school holidays, working under the direct supervision of Mrs Bailey, the manageress.'

'Terrific . . .' I murmured. I stood there in a daze for a moment, and then I thought quickly and whispered something to him behind my hand.

'Of course,' he said when I'd finished, 'and that's a very kindly thought, young Katie.'

He spoke into the microphone again. 'Ladies and gentlemen, if only all young people were as unselfish and thoughtful as Katie! As the judging was so close, she has requested that the first prize should be split and her runner-up should receive part of it. Katie, therefore, will get the book tokens and Antonia will be the lucky girl who'll receive the week's work experience in After Six Cocktail and Continental Cruise Wear!'

To tumultuous applause, I sat down.

'Well!' Mrs Bayleaf said.

'How very noble of you,' said Helen.

'Ah yes. A completely unselfish gesture,' Mum

said, giving me one of her looks.

I smiled my best, most generous and loving smile. 'I thought it was the least I could do,' I said. 'After all, she *is* my best friend.'

Find out how Katie survived
her first encounter with the
extraordinary Mrs Bayleaf in

THE REVOLTING
BRIDESMAID

MARY HOOPER

AVAILABLE NOW
Turn the page for a sneak preview . . .

BLOOMSBURY

chapter one

I slid down the stairs and was about to do a forward roll into the sitting room when Mum ran into the hall and more or less threw herself across the door to stop me going in.

'Don't go in there now!' she said, waving her hands about and pulling a peculiar face. 'It's

Helen and Christopher!' And then she mouthed something excitedly and pulled me into the kitchen.

I looked at her in concern; she appeared to have gone quite loopy. 'Helen's doing what?' I asked.

'Sssh,' Mum said. 'She and Christopher are talking to Dad now. You know how he likes things to be done properly, your dad.'

'Helen and That Man,' I said in a louder voice, 'are doing *what*?'

'Sshh,' Mum said again, sitting down on the edge of the kitchen table. 'Getting married! People do, you know.'

'Not in this house they don't,' I said, amazed and a bit put out because I'd been the last to know something important again. 'Not often.'

'No, not often,' Mum said, 'just sometimes — and I do hope you're not going to be difficult, Katie. You must have seen the signs, after all.'

'What signs?'

'That she and Christopher were serious about each other, of course.'

Signs? I thought hard but couldn't remember seeing any. Real signs? Black and white HELEN

AND CHRISTOPHER ARE SERIOUS signs? I hadn't seen any of those.

Anyway, even if I had . . . I didn't exactly fancy the idea. OK, it would be nice to have Mum and Dad all to myself, but sometimes Helen could be fun. *And* she gave me her old make-up and clothes. Also, if she wasn't around I'd have to have old Mrs Crabbe down the road to babysit all the time. Besides, I certainly didn't want her to marry *him*. She'd been out with much nicer ones. He was too old for a start, and he wore old-fashioned trousers and stupid shirts patterned with little

cars or little trees. Worst of all, he was a teacher and kept asking me things about school in a bracing voice, like: 'How's the old history project going?' or, last week, on seeing me throwing my maths homework into the bin in disgust, 'In trouble with our binary numbers, are we?'

I tiptoed out of the kitchen and dropped on to all fours in front of the sitting-room door to try and listen to what was going on.

'Come away from that door at once!' Mum hissed from the kitchen. 'How's it going to look when they open it and you're kneeling there with

your ears flapping?'

'I'm not. I'm just sitting here examining the world of nature beneath the edge of this carpet,' I said. 'There's a little tiny thing with two hundred legs, a black beetle – well, half of one – a –'

'Come away from that door *now*!' Mum said sternly, but not before I heard him – That Man – saying something boring about mortgages and putting down deposits.

I reluctantly rolled over towards her and she looked at me and shook her head wearily. 'Now, before they come out, why don't you go upstairs and put on something other than that dreadful old tracksuit?'

'You bought this dreadful old tracksuit,' I pointed out. 'You wanted me to have one.'

'I didn't know you'd wear it day in and day out. It was clean when I bought it. Clean and pale pink,' she said with a sigh, 'and now it always seems to be grey.'

'She can't marry him!' I said urgently, ignoring the insults to my tracksuit. 'He's too old, for a start. He doesn't look like a bridegroom.'

'What do they look like, then?'

I thought back to a black and white film I'd seen on TV on Sunday afternoon. 'They're good-looking — like film stars — with slicked-back black hair and shiny shoes. They've got a bouquet of flowers in one hand and a diamond ring in a little box in the other.'

'I can't see any diamond rings forthcoming,' Mum said. 'Not on what he earns. And people don't have shiny shoes any more.'

'But he's old . . .' I wailed. 'Horribly old and fat.'

'Don't be silly,' Mum said. 'He's not at all fat. His face is chubby, that's all. And he's only twenty-nine.'

'That's what he tells you,' I said darkly.

'And Helen's twenty-two. That's a good age difference.'

'Fat, old and boring,' I said stubbornly. Of all the interesting people I could have had for a brother-in-law, I had to be lumbered with *him*.

'You'll not be losing a sister; you're gaining a brother,' Mum said.

'I don't want to gain a brother,' I said, infuriated. 'Not a brother like *him*, anyway. If she's got to

get married, then why can't it be someone in the royal family, or a pop star, or a DJ or someone exciting. Not him; *definitely* not him.'

'Well, I'm afraid it's not up to you,' she said. 'When you get married you're allowed to choose for yourself and I must say Dad and I are very —'

The sitting-room door handle rattled and Mum broke off and looked towards it expectantly, and then Helen and That Man came out holding hands and looking at each other with very silly grins.

'It's OK,' Helen said to Mum, smiling a big soppy smile. 'It's all arranged.'

'As if I actually had any say in the matter!' Dad shouted in a jolly voice, and then I heard glasses tinkling and he came through into the kitchen with a bottle of something on a tray.

I looked at That Man stonily: at his horrible shirt, silly trousers and face with a stupid pleased expression on it. The shame of it; imagine having to tell everyone that Helen was marrying *him*. I mean, couldn't she find anyone better? Surely she couldn't be that desperate?

I looked at Helen: she wasn't bad . . . she had frizzy red hair and lots of freckles and she dressed quite nicely . . . so was this frump in peculiar trousers honestly all she could get? But perhaps she hadn't looked properly; perhaps she needed a helping hand. Maybe it wasn't too late to find her someone better . . .

'Katie!' Mum said suddenly. 'How about having a little sip of something to celebrate?'

'And how about a kiss for your new brother?' That Man said heartily.

I screwed up my face in absolute disgust.

'Oh, Katie never kisses anyone,' Mum said hastily, moving to stand between him and my face.

'We've got another surprise for you!' Helen said, obviously not caring that she was leaning cosily against a shirt patterned with tiny fire engines. 'Something you've always wanted.'

'Not Disneyland?' I squealed. Maybe they were going there on honeymoon and taking me . . . if so, it wasn't too late for us to become instant best friends.

They laughed. 'Not quite that,' Helen said. 'The wedding will be quite soon – in September – and we want you to be our bridesmaid.'

'Yuk!' I said.